Date: 3/20/18

J 796.35764 BRA
Braun, Eric,
Pro baseball's underdogs :
players and teams who

PALM BEACH COUNTY
LIBRARY SYSTEM
3650 SUMMIT BLVD.
WEST PALM BEACH, FL 33406

PRO BASEBALL'S UNDERDOGS:
PLAYERS AND TEAMS WHO SHOCKED THE BASEBALL WORLD

BY ERIC BRAUN

CAPSTONE PRESS
a capstone imprint

Sports Illustrated Kids Sports Shockers! are published by Capstone Press,
1710 Roe Crest Drive, North Mankato, Minnesota 56003
www.mycapstone.com

Copyright © 2018 by Capstone Press, a Capstone imprint. All rights reserved.
No part of this publication may be reproduced in whole or in part, or stored in a
retrieval system, or transmitted in any form or by any means, electronic, mechanical,
photocopying, recording, or otherwise, without written permission of the publisher.

Sports Illustrated Kids is a trademark of Time Inc. Used with permission.

Library of Congress Cataloging-in-Publication data
Names: Braun, Eric, 1971- author. Title: Pro baseball's underdogs : players and
teams who shocked the baseball world / by Eric Braun. Description: North
Mankato, Minnesota : Capstone Press, 2017. | Series: Sports Illustrated Kids. Sports
Shockers! Identifiers: LCCN 2017004651 (print) | LCCN 2017010568 (ebook) | ISBN
9781515780519 (eBook PDF) | ISBN 9781515780472 (library binding) Subjects: LCSH:
Baseball—United States—History—Juvenile literature. | Baseball players—United
States—Biography—Juvenile literature. Classification: LCC GV863.A1 (ebook) | LCC
GV863.A1 B73 2017 (print) | DDC 796.357/64—dc23 LC record available at https://
lccn.loc.gov/2017004651

Editorial Credits
Nick Healy, editor; Kyle Grenz, designer; Eric Gohl, media researcher;
Kathy McColley, production specialist

Photo Credits
AP Photo: 16; Dreamstime: Jerry Coli, 11; Getty Images: Bettmann, 27, New York Daily
News Archive, 13, Sports Illustrated/Walter Iooss Jr., 12; iStockphoto: 4x6, cover (left);
Newscom: UPI/Pat Benic, 17, UPI/Ray Stubblebine, 6–7 (bottom), USA Today Sports/
Anthony Gruppuso, 7 (top), ZUMA Press/St Petersburg Times, 26; Shutterstock:
Beto Chagas, cover (right); Sports Illustrated: Al Tielemans, 28, 30 (bottom), Chuck
Solomon, 18, 22, David E. Klutho, 19, Heinz Kluetmeier, 21 (all), John Biever, 14, 15,
29, John G. Zimmerman, 31 (bottom), John Iacono, 10, 20, 23, 24, 25, Robert Beck, 4, 5,
Simon Bruty, 8, 9, Tony Triolo, 30 (top), Walter Iooss Jr., 31 (top)

```
Printed and bound in the USA.
010364F17
```

Table of Contents

Baseball's Underdogs 4
The Royal Treatment 6
Rise of the Thing 8
Quick Switch for Success 10
Amazin' Mets 12
Diamondbacks Shine 14
Lovable Losers 16
Big Man Makes It Big 18
Worst to First 20
The Unwanted Slugger 22
Dodgers Ride a Golden Arm 24
An Old Rookie 26
They Might Be Giants 28
Underdog Roundup 30

Read More 32
Internet Sites 32
Index 32

Baseball's UNDERDOGS

What makes underdog stories so fun? Unless our favorite team is expected to win, most of us love to see an upset. It's surprising. It's exciting. It reminds us that anything is possible.

Take the Kansas City Royals. In nearly 30 years preceding 2014, they lost more baseball games than any other team. They made the playoffs exactly zero times. Think about that: three decades of losing.

Three decades of bad baseball.

Then came 2014, when the Royals squeaked into the playoffs as a wild-card team. Few thought the team would get far, though. After all, they had little power and a starting rotation that was less than dominant.

What they did have was killer defense and an airtight bullpen. They rode that magical combination to a sweep of the playoffs and a date with San Francisco in the World Series.

The Giants had won two of the last four championships, and the Royals were underdogs. In the end, KC lost in seven games, but 2014 went down as one of the most entertaining World Series ever. A big reason for that was seeing the underdogs fight their way to the very end.

Major League Baseball (MLB) is loaded with thrilling underdog tales, from scrappy players to never-say-die teams.

They all have two things in common:

THE ROYALS HADN'T PLAYED IN THE WORLD SERIES SINCE THEIR 1985 CLUB DEFEATED THE ST. LOUIS CARDINALS IN SEVEN GAMES.

THEY SUCCEEDED AGAINST ALL ODDS, AND THEY WERE DARN FUN TO WATCH.

SPOILER ALERT: THE ROYALS WOULD BE BACK IN 2015, AND THEY'D BE EVEN BETTER.

The ROYAL Treatment

The rallying Royals of 2014 pushed the World Series all the way to Game 7 before losing a classic. The following year, many expected Kansas City to sink back toward the bottom in the standings. Surely they had used up all their magic on that near-miss against the Giants. But KC still had a great bullpen. They still had a top-ranked defense. Their hitters might not have had a ton of power, but they could slap the ball around the field.

The Royals fought their way back to the World Series. They faced the New York Mets, a team featuring four starters who could throw 95 miles per hour. That's serious heat. And the Mets lineup launched lots of homers. Once again the Royals were the underdogs. But KC took the first two games at home. They lost Game 3 in New York, but clutch hitting and that lights-out bullpen helped them nail down Game 4.

ERIC HOSMER'S AGGRESSIVE BASE RUNNING HELPED CARRY THE ROYALS TO A TITLE.

FACT: IN THE 2015 POSTSEASON, THE ROYALS WON A REMARKABLE SEVEN GAMES IN WHICH THEY TRAILED BY TWO OR MORE RUNS. THE PREVIOUS RECORD WAS FIVE GAMES.

In Game 5 the Mets took a 2-0 lead into the ninth inning. KC clawed back to tie the game courtesy of some daring base running by Eric Hosmer. He danced off third base as Mets' third-bagger David Wright fielded a grounder. Wright began his throw to first, and Hosmer broke for home. First baseman Lucas Duda caught Wright's throw for the second out of the inning and fired to the plate. Hosmer slid in safe.

That tied the game, and the Royals eventually won in 12 innings. They claimed the World Series championship for the first time since 1985 and only the second time in club history.

THE ROYALS CELEBRATE AFTER DEFEATING THE METS TO CLAIM THE 2015 CHAMPIONSHIP.

RISE of the THING

R.A. Dickey was drafted in the first round in 1996 by the Texas Rangers. The hard-throwing college pitcher was promised a hefty signing bonus, and his future looked bright. But when team doctors examined his arm, they found he had a missing ligament. That's right: An entire ligament was just not there. He'd been born without it, and no one had ever known.

The team didn't pay the promised bonus. After all, doctors assumed he would never make it as a big leaguer. They were surprised he could even throw at all. In spite of that, Dickey was a solid pitcher in the minors and occasionally the majors. Not great, but okay. He threw a decent fastball and decent breaking ball. He also had one weird pitch he called "The Thing."

He spent a few years bouncing from team to team, from minors to majors, from rotation to bullpen.

Then Dickey went from decent to not so good. He needed to make a change if he wanted to stick in the majors. That's when he started throwing The Thing full time. What he didn't know was that The Thing was actually a hard knuckleball. It saved his career.

R.A. DICKEY'S KNUCKLEBALL GRIP

Big league hitters had a hard time getting solid contact with the dancing knuckler. He also could pitch on back-to-back days, which was valuable. His arm didn't get sore. Pitching for the New York Mets in 2012, Dickey threw 233.2 innings with five complete games. He struck out 230 batters and won the Cy Young Award.

Earlier that year, Dickey wrote an autobiography. In it, he revealed that he had been sexually abused as a young boy. As an adult, he struggled with depression and suicidal thoughts. Dickey had been an underdog in more ways than one. His grit and love of the game helped him overcome many challenges.

FACT: PHIL NIEKRO WON 318 GAMES, THE MOST BY A KNUCKLEBALL PITCHER IN MLB HISTORY. HIS BROTHER JOE NIEKRO, ALSO A KNUCKLE-CHUCKER, WON 221. THAT GIVES THE BROTHERS 539 KNUCKLEBALL WINS.

QUICK SWITCH for SUCCESS

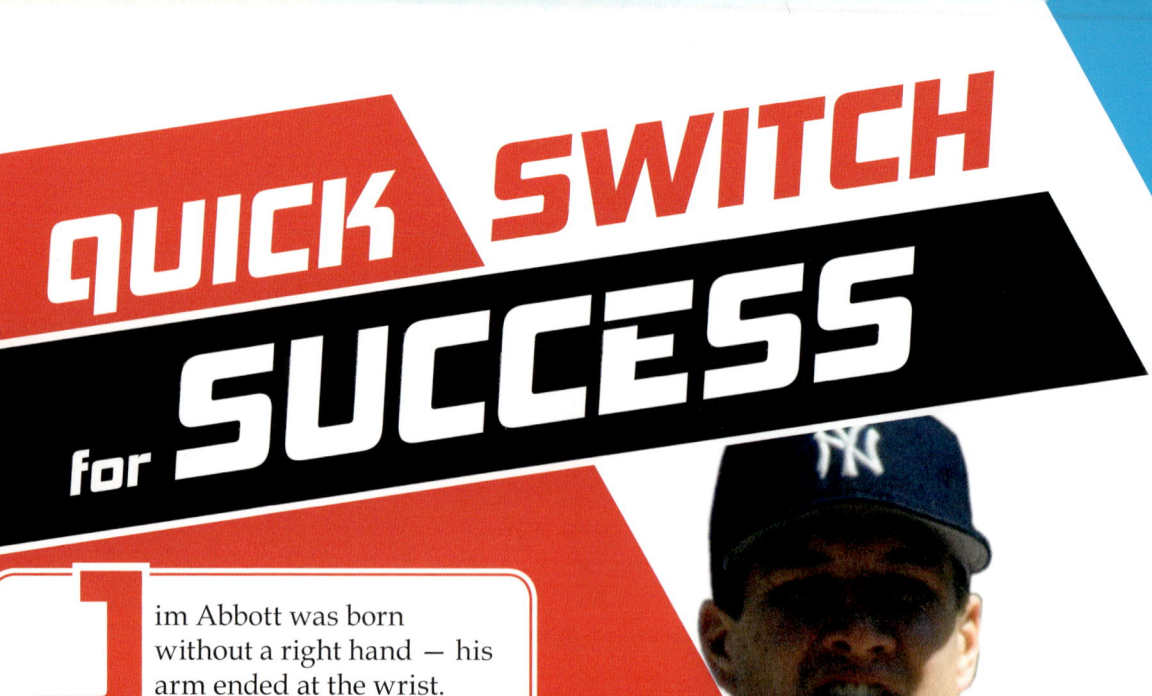

Jim Abbott was born without a right hand — his arm ended at the wrist. When he was young, his parents encouraged him to do what he wanted and not let his disability stop him. What he wanted was to play baseball. But how do you play baseball with one hand?

Abbott trained himself by throwing a rubber ball against a wall. He started with his glove on his right wrist. He threw the ball with his left hand. Then he jammed his left hand into the glove so he could field the ball when it bounced back. As he got better at the quick switch, he moved closer and closer to the wall. That made him switch quicker and quicker.

ABBOTT PLAYED FOR FIVE CLUBS, INCLUDING THE YANKEES IN 1993 AND 1994.

FACT:
ABBOTT WENT 18-11 IN 1991 WITH A SPARKLING 2.89 ERA. HE CAME IN THIRD IN CY YOUNG VOTING. ROGER CLEMENS WON IT THAT YEAR, HIS THIRD CY YOUNG.

At age 11, he joined a Little League team. He threw a no-hitter in the first game he pitched. He played in high school and college. Every step of the way, he succeeded. Batters often tried bunting on him, thinking he couldn't switch his glove fast enough. But he almost always fielded the bunt and threw the runner out.

ABBOTT SIGNED WITH THE CALIFORNIA ANGELS IN 1988. HE MADE THE TEAM IN 1989 AND WON ROOKIE OF THE YEAR. HIS MLB CAREER SPANNED 10 YEARS, AND HE WON 87 GAMES.

AMAZIN' METS

NOLAN RYAN BRINGS THE HEAT AGAINST THE ORIOLES IN THE 1969 WORLD SERIES.

The New York Mets debuted in MLB in 1962 and lost 120 games. They lost at least 100 games five times in their first seven seasons. To say they were bad would be like saying ice is cold. Being bad was their most obvious trait.

But in 1969 something changed. Anchored by two future Hall of Famers, right-handers Tom Seaver and Nolan Ryan, their youthful pitching staff suffocated opposing offenses. Manager Gil Hodges got his players to buy into a team-first philosophy. Things began to break their way. People started calling them the Amazin' Mets.

After beating the Atlanta Braves in the National League Championship Series (NLCS), they faced the powerful Baltimore Orioles in the World Series. Baltimore was the best team of the era. They had won 109 regular season games. But the Amazin' Mets shocked Baltimore and won the championship.

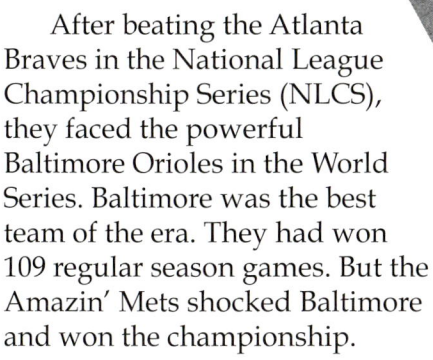

The miracle of the Mets' win was captured perfectly in one play. Infielder Al Weiss, who hit a grand total of seven home runs in his entire career, blasted a Game 5 pitch deep into the outfield. He ran as hard as he could, thinking he might have a double. Then he realized he had more than that.

"I started hearing the crowd roar and thought something must have happened," he later said. "I guess I don't know how to react to a home run."

The Mets may not have known how to react to being baseball's champs, but they figured it out.

VICTORIOUS PITCHER JERRY KOOSMAN LEAPED INTO THE ARMS OF CATCHER JERRY GROTE AS FANS AT NEW YORK'S SHEA STADIUM WENT WILD.

FACT: THE METS' NOLAN RYAN WAS ONLY 22 YEARS OLD IN 1969, BUT HE BECAME ONE OF THE MOST DOMINANT PITCHERS OF ALL TIME. HE PLAYED FOR 27 YEARS AND WON 324 GAMES. HE STRUCK OUT 5,714 BATTERS, BY FAR THE MOST IN MLB HISTORY.

Diamondbacks SHINE

In the late 1990s, one team stood above all the rest. The New York Yankees won four out of the five World Series from 1996 to 2000. They were stacked with stars, including shortstop Derek Jeter, centerfielder Bernie Williams, and catcher Jorge Posada.

Their most important star may have been Mariano Rivera. He was turning out to be the greatest relief pitcher of all time. His best pitch — the cutter — broke bats as if they were matchsticks. The pitch put fear into the hearts of grown men. Nicknamed "Sandman," Rivera had finished 23 straight postseason saves without blowing a lead. If New York handed him a lead at the end of a game, that game was over. Turn out the lights, and go home.

On the other hand, the Arizona Diamondbacks were an expansion team, having joined the league in 1998. The D-Backs hadn't even existed when New York started its run of championships in 1996.

MARIANO RIVERA TRIED TO CLOSE OUT THE D-BACKS AND CLAIM YET ANOTHER TITLE FOR NEW YORK.

LUIS GONZALEZ KNOCKED 57 HOMERS DURING THE REGULAR SEASON BUT WON IT ALL WITH AN OPPOSITE-FIELD FLARE.

Yet there the Diamondbacks were, playing in the 2001 World Series. They pushed the Yankees all the way to Game 7. In the bottom of the ninth inning, the Yankees led the Diamondbacks 2–1, and Sandman took the mound.

GULP.

Diamondbacks first baseman Mark Grace led off with a single. To see Rivera give up even one hit was shocking. But then Tony Womack doubled down the right-field line to tie the game. Even more shocking.

Finally, slugger Luis Gonzalez drove in the winning run with a blooper over short. While the Diamondbacks celebrated on the field, Rivera walked off with his head hanging.

SHOCKING.

FACT:
ARIZONA WON A WORLD SERIES FASTER THAN ANY OTHER EXPANSION TEAM. THEY DID IT IN THEIR FOURTH SEASON. THE FLORIDA MARLINS DID IT IN FIVE SEASONS, AND THE NEW YORK METS DID IT IN EIGHT.

Lovable LOSERS

The 2016 Chicago Cubs might not have seemed like underdogs. They were favored to win the World Series from day one of spring training. They charged through the regular season, winning 103 games. And they won a dramatic World Series, capped by a thrilling 10-inning Game 7.

But before all that, they were the biggest losers in all of baseball. They owned the longest championship drought in pro sports: Their last title came in 1908.

SOME FANS CLAIMED THE CUBS WERE CURSED. THEY HAD MADE THE PLAYOFFS A HANDFUL OF TIMES OVER THE DECADES, BUT THEY ALWAYS FOUND A WAY TO BLOW IT. EACH TIME THEY DID, THE LEGEND OF THE LOVABLE LOSERS GREW.

IN 1984 THE CUBS INVITED TAVERN OWNER SAM SIANIS AND HIS GOAT TO A PLAYOFF GAME. THE ATTEMPT TO BREAK A SUPPOSED CURSE ON THE TEAM DID NOT WORK.

And they were loved. Cubs fans bonded in their belief that someday, someday, the team would win it all. In a weird way, losing and waiting — and hoping — was a big part of the fun.

Then came 2016, when they faced the Cleveland Indians in the World Series. Fielding the final ground ball in Game 7, Cubs third baseman Kris Bryant smiled wildly. He knew this was it. He scooped up the ball and threw to first.

GAME OVER. SERIES OVER. CURSE OVER.

What happens now? After 108 years of waiting, will the magic of being a Cubs fan fade? Maybe winning a couple more championships will help.

LONGEST TITLE DROUGHTS IN PRO SPORTS

ARIZONA CARDINALS, NFL, 1947 (69 YEARS)
CLEVELAND INDIANS, MLB, 1948 (68 YEARS)
SACRAMENTO KINGS, NBA, 1951 (65 YEARS)
DETROIT LIONS, NFL, 1957 (59 YEARS)
ATLANTA HAWKS, NBA, 1958 (58 YEARS)
MINNESOTA VIKINGS, NFL, NEVER (56 YEARS)
PHILADELPHIA EAGLES, NFL, 1960 (56 YEARS)
HOUSTON ASTROS, MLB, NEVER (55 YEARS)

Note: Pro football's Cardinals were based in St. Louis when they won in 1947. Pro basketball's Kings were based in Rochester, N.Y., and called the Royals when they won in 1951. Basketball's Hawks were based in St. Louis when they won in 1958.

Big Man MAKES IT BIG

HERE IS A MAN WHO, FOR SEVERAL YEARS, WAS THE BEST PLAYER IN BASEBALL. EASILY.

Even as a kid in the Dominican Republic, Albert Pujols was big and strong and hit baseballs very far. But Major League teams weren't interested in drafting him.

For one thing, teams worried that he was too big and bulky to play defense in the big leagues. Another issue was his age. How could someone so big and so good really be so young? Some scouts believed he must be lying about his age and his career would end sooner than expected.

The St. Louis Cardinals finally drafted Albert Pujols in the 13th round in 1999. Pujols, who had recently gotten married, considered giving up baseball so he could take a job and support his family. Lucky for him — and for the Cards — he decided to play.

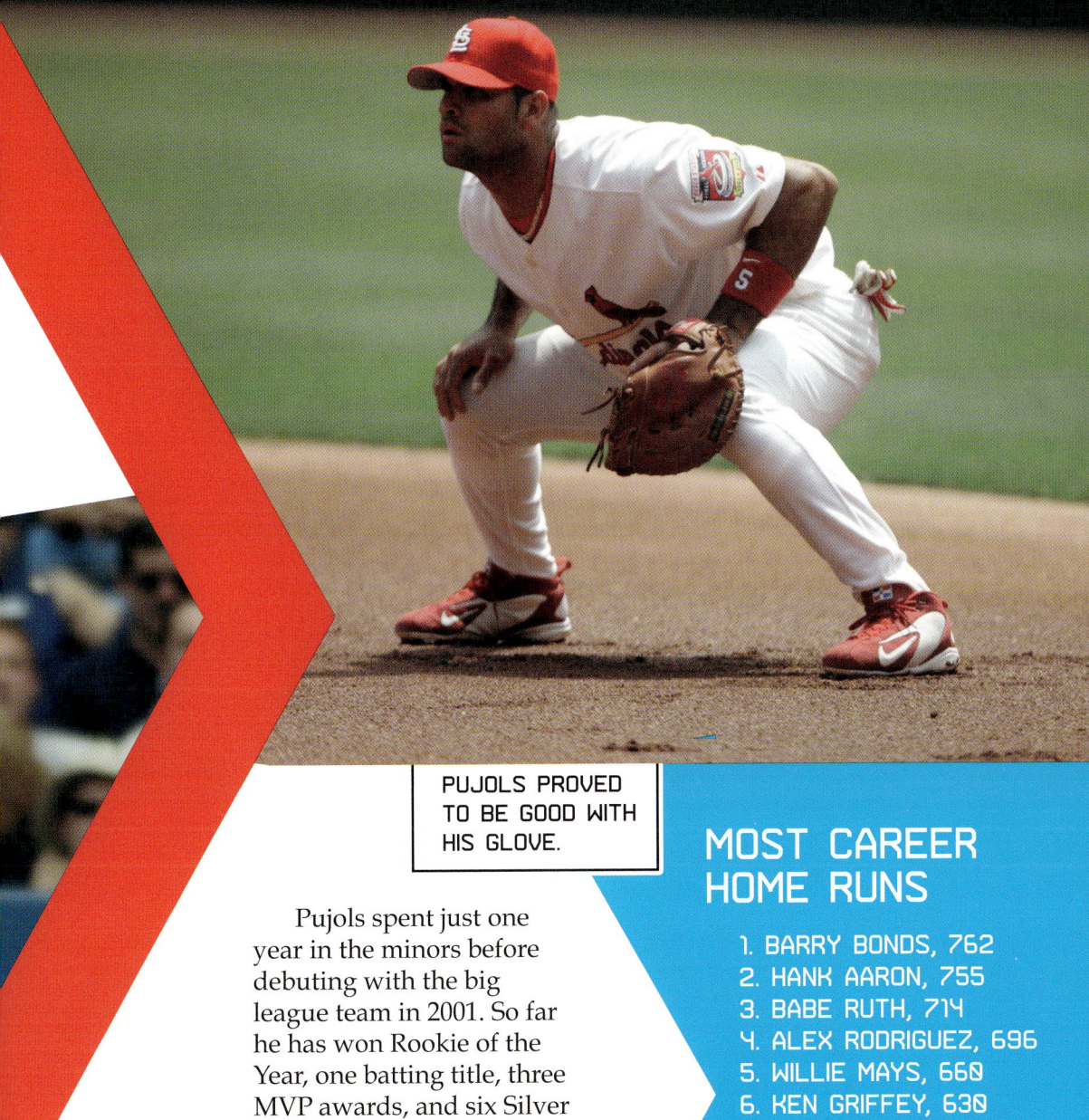

PUJOLS PROVED TO BE GOOD WITH HIS GLOVE.

Pujols spent just one year in the minors before debuting with the big league team in 2001. So far he has won Rookie of the Year, one batting title, three MVP awards, and six Silver Sluggers. He and the Cards went to three World Series, winning two of them. In his first 16 seasons in the majors, he hit 591 home runs for the Cardinals and the Angels.

MOST CAREER HOME RUNS

1. BARRY BONDS, 762
2. HANK AARON, 755
3. BABE RUTH, 714
4. ALEX RODRIGUEZ, 696
5. WILLIE MAYS, 660
6. KEN GRIFFEY, 630
7. JIM THOME, 612
8. SAMMY SOSA, 609
9. ALBERT PUJOLS, 591*
10. FRANK ROBINSON, 586

* through 2016

OH, AND ABOUT THAT DEFENSE: HE HAS WON TWO GOLD GLOVES.

Worst to FIRST

IS IT POSSIBLE FOR TWO TEAMS TO BOTH BE UNDERDOGS IN THE SAME WORLD SERIES?

The Atlanta Braves and the Minnesota Twins both finished last in their divisions in 1990. These teams weren't just bad. Atlanta had the worst record in the game. Minnesota was only a bit better. No team had ever made the World Series one year after finishing last. Amazingly, in 1991 both these teams did.

It turned out to be one of the most gripping fall classics ever played. Three of the seven games went into extra innings. Four ended on walk-offs. Five were decided by one run.

In Game 6, with the Twins down three games to two, Minnesota outfielder Kirby Puckett practically won the game on his own. He soared into the wall in left-center to rob Atlanta of an extra-base hit, and he drove in two runs and scored another. Then, in the bottom of the 11th, he hit a homer to win it and force Game 7.

KIRBY PUCKETT AFTER HITTING THE GAME-WINNER IN GAME 6

LONNIE SMITH WAS OUT ON THIS PLAY AT THE PLATE IN GAME 4, BUT THE BRAVES TOOK GAMES 3, 4, AND 5 AT HOME.

This Series was so exciting, Puckett's Game 6 was only the second-greatest performance. It was topped the following night when Twins pitcher Jack Morris tossed 10 shutout innings to win it all.

JACK MORRIS PITCHED OUT OF A JAM IN THE EIGHTH INNING AND LASTED THROUGH 10 TO BEAT THE BRAVES IN GAME 7.

FACT: WHAT COULD BE MORE THRILLING THAN PITCHING A 10-INNING SHUTOUT TO WIN THE WORLD SERIES? DOING IT FOR YOUR HOMETOWN TEAM. JACK MORRIS GREW UP IN ST. PAUL, MINNESOTA, DREAMING OF WINNING IT ALL WITH THE TWINS.

The UNWANTED Slugger

In college in 1986, Mike Piazza almost walked away from baseball. No MLB team had selected him in the draft. He almost walked away again two years later, after the Dodgers finally drafted him with the 1,390th pick.

The Dodgers ignored him after the draft. They didn't offer him a contract. They didn't even call, because they never intended to sign him. Turns out they had drafted him only as a favor to their manager, Tommy Lasorda. He was a family friend of the Piazzas.

Months later, Lasorda convinced the team to sign Piazza. The team's front office agreed, but Piazza would have to learn a new position — catcher.

"THEY NEVER WANTED HIM," LASORDA LATER SAID. "THEY HELD IT AGAINST HIM BECAUSE OF MY RELATIONSHIP WITH HIM."

MOST HOME RUNS AS A CATCHER, CAREER

1. MIKE PIAZZA, 396
2. CARLTON FISK, 351
3. JOHNNY BENCH, 327
4. YOGI BERRA, 305
5. LANCE PARRISH, 299

While Piazza was in Class A minor league ball, he finally walked away. He told the Dodgers he quit. Learning to play catcher was too hard, and the game was no longer fun for him.

Lucky for him, he changed his mind days later. It was lucky for fans too, because Piazza went on to become the greatest hitting catcher of all time. He hit 427 career home runs, including 396 as a catcher before moving to first base. That's the MLB record for that position. He was inducted into the Hall of Fame in 2016.

Dodgers Ride a GOLDEN ARM

Sportscaster Bob Costas called the 1988 Dodgers' offense the worst lineup in World Series history. The Dodgers had won only 73 games the year before and had lots of holes on the roster.

So how did they get there? And how did they win? The biggest reason is probably pitcher Orel Hershiser.

Hershiser had been considered reliable—not really an ace.

BUT IN 1988 HE PITCHED LIKE AN ACE.

He went 23–8 and led the National League in wins, shutouts, and innings pitched. He polished off the regular season by tossing a mind-boggling 59 consecutive scoreless innings.

In the NLCS against the Mets, Hershiser handed leads to the bullpen in games 1 and 3, only to see his relievers blow it. He came back and saved Game 4 and fired a five-hit shutout in Game 7.

The Dodgers limped into the World Series. Injuries hampered MVP outfielder Kirk Gibson as well as catcher Mike Scioscia and star pitcher Fernando Valenzuela. Their opponents, the Oakland Athletics, were a powerhouse. They featured the famous "Bash Brothers," Jose Canseco and Mark McGwire. The two sluggers combined for 74 homers that year.

The Dodgers shut them down, though. Hershiser tossed a three-hitter and a four-hitter in his two World Series wins.

KIRK GIBSON BATTED ONLY ONCE IN THE 1988 WORLD SERIES, DUE TO KNEE AND HAMSTRING INJURIES.

FACT: KIRK GIBSON LIMPED TO THE PLATE TO PINCH HIT IN THE NINTH INNING OF GAME 1. OAKLAND'S STAR CLOSER, DENNIS ECKERSLEY, WAS PROTECTING A ONE-RUN LEAD. GIBSON BLASTED A TWO-RUN HOMER TO WIN THE GAME. HE HOBBLED AROUND THE BASES, MAKING WORLD SERIES HISTORY.

An OLD Rookie

Back in 1983, pitcher Jim Morris seemed to be on his way to a successful baseball career. He had been drafted fourth overall by the Milwaukee Brewers. But a series of arm injuries forced him to quit the game. Instead of playing ball, he got his college degree and became a high school science teacher and baseball coach.

Years later, Morris gave a speech to his high school team about the importance of dreams and hard work. His players had a question for their coach: What about your dream of playing Major League Baseball?

WHEN HE FINALLY MADE IT TO THE BIGS, MORRIS STRUCK OUT THE FIRST BATTER HE FACED.

MORRIS MADE A DEAL WITH THE TEAM. IF THEY WON THEIR DISTRICT CHAMPIONSHIP, HE WOULD TRY OUT FOR A BIG LEAGUE TEAM.

FACT: ALTHOUGH 35 IS VERY OLD FOR AN MLB DEBUT, MORRIS WAS NOT THE OLDEST ROOKIE EVER. IN FACT, AT LEAST A COUPLE DOZEN PLAYERS WERE OLDER. THE MOST FAMOUS MIGHT BE SATCHEL PAIGE, WHO HAD A LONG CAREER IN THE NEGRO LEAGUES BEFORE DEBUTING IN MLB AT AGE 42.

His team did win the title, and Morris kept his promise by trying out for the Tampa Bay Devil Rays. He was surprised to find that he could pitch 98 miles per hour. At 35 years old, an age when many players are retiring, Jim Morris signed with Tampa Bay. On September 18, 1999, he made his major league debut. A shoulder injury in 2000 interfered with his brief career. He ended up making 21 big league appearances before retiring in 2001.

AFTER FINDING OUT HE WAS THROWING 98 MILES PER HOUR, MORRIS LATER APOLOGIZED TO HIS HIGH SCHOOL PLAYERS. HE HADN'T REALIZED HOW HARD HE WAS THROWING TO THEM DURING BATTING PRACTICE.

Morris wrote a book about his experience called *The Oldest Rookie*. His story became the 2002 movie *The Rookie*, which starred Dennis Quaid as the aging pitcher.

LEROY ROBERT "SATCHEL" PAIGE WAS INDUCTED INTO THE HALL OF FAME IN 1971.

They MIGHT Be GIANTS

On August 29, 2010, with about a month of the regular season left, the San Francisco Giants were five games out of first place. The Giants had not won a title since 1954, four years before the franchise had moved to San Francisco from New York.

Few considered them World Series contenders in 2010. Their catcher and cleanup hitter, Buster Posey, had started the season in the minors. Outfielder Pat Burrell had been released by Tampa Bay. Another outfielder, Cody Ross, was claimed on waivers. They were a ragtag collection of misfits and castoffs.

THE 2010 GIANTS BEAT THE RANGERS FOUR GAMES TO ONE.

"WE'VE BEEN GETTING OVERLOOKED A LOT," SAID CLOSER BRIAN WILSON. "BUT THAT'S JUST FINE."

TIM LINCECUM

The strength of the team was an exciting core of young pitchers. They included four homegrown starters—Tim Lincecum, Matt Cain, Jonathan Sanchez, and Madison Bumgarner. As the calendar flipped to September, those pitchers went 22–8 with a 2.02 ERA to finish the season. The pitchers carried their team to a division title. They knocked off two-time defending National League champs Philadelphia in the NLCS and faced the Texas Rangers in the World Series.

FACT: TO BEAT THE RANGERS, THE GIANTS HAD TO BEAT 2008 CY YOUNG WINNER CLIFF LEE TWICE.

To win the first World Series title in San Francisco history, they would have to shut down a powerful Texas lineup. No problem. Cain and Bumgarner both tossed shutouts. The Rangers hit .190 as a team in the Series, and at one point they failed to score for 18 $\frac{1}{3}$ straight innings. It took 56 years, but finally the San Francisco Giants were the champs.

Underdog ROUNDUP

Jim Eisenreich: In 1982 this talented outfielder seemed like a star in the making. Then he was forced to quit the game because of Tourette's syndrome. The disorder of the nervous system causes repeated, involuntarily bodily movements and sounds. He missed all or part of several years before an amazing comeback. With treatment for his illness, Eisenreich put together a career that spanned 15 big league seasons and included World Series appearances with the Phillies and Marlins.

David Eckstein: This undersized infielder hit for average and little else. Labeled as "scrappy" throughout his career, he went 8 for 13 for the Cardinals in the final three games of the 2006 World Series. His Cards beat the Tigers, and he won the series MVP award.

Tim Lincecum: He was a dominant high school and college pitcher. Still, big league teams considered him too small to endure the heavy workload of pro baseball. But with unique pitching mechanics invented by his dad, Lincecum was able to hit the high 90s with his fastball and toss a devastating curve. Size was not a problem for "The Freak." He won two Cy Young Awards and three championships with the San Francisco Giants.

Tommy John: On July 17, 1974, at age 31, John felt something pop in his arm while he was throwing a pitch. It turned out that his ulnar collateral ligament had been destroyed. Faced with the prospect of never pitching again, John tried something brave and radical for his time. He became the first pitcher in history to have the ligament in his pitching elbow replaced with a ligament taken from elsewhere in his body. John went on to pitch 15 more years. The surgery he had is now common for pitchers and bears his name: Tommy John surgery.

1960

Pittsburgh Pirates: The Pirates' opponents in the World Series, the New York Yankees, had won six titles in the 1950s. The Yanks were heavily favored to win again. But the Pirates toppled them, highlighted by Bill Mazeroski's thrilling homer in the bottom of the ninth in Game 7 to clinch it.

2016

Cleveland Indians: They lost several key players to injury: All-Star outfielder Michael Brantley, starting catcher Yan Gomes, and two of their top three starting pitchers, Carlos Carrasco and Danny Salazar. Yet they jumped to a three-games-to-one lead over the Cubs in the World Series and pushed the contest to extra innings in Game 7 before losing. Cleveland owns the longest championship drought in North American sports — 68 years.

READ MORE

Braun, Eric. *Baseball Stats and the Stories Behind Them: What Every Fan Needs to Know*. North Mankato, Minn.: Capstone Press, 2016.

Editors of Sports Illustrated Kids. *Baseball: Then to WOW!* New York: Sports Illustrated, 2016.

Hetrick, Hans. *Baseball's Record Breakers*. North Mankato, Minn.: Capstone Press, 2017.

INTERNET SITES

Use FactHound to find Internet sites related to this book.

Visit www.facthound.com

Just type in 9781515780472 and go.

INDEX

Abbott, Jim, 10-11
Angels, 11, 19
Arizona Diamondbacks, 14-15
Atlanta Braves, 13, 20-21

Baltimore Orioles, 13
Bryant, Kris, 17
Bumgarner, Madison, 29

Cain, Matt, 29
Chicago Cubs, 16-17, 31
Cleveland Indians, 17, 31

Dickey, R.A., 8-9
Duda, Lucas, 7

Eckstein, David, 30
Eisenreich, Jim, 30

Gibson, Kirk, 25
Gonzalez, Luis, 15
Grote, Jerry, 13

Hershiser, Orel, 24-25
Hodges, Gil, 12
Hosmer, Eric, 4, 7

Jeter, Derek, 14
John, Tommy, 31

Kansas City Royals, 4-5, 6-7
Koosman, Jerry, 13

Lincecum, Tim, 29, 30
Los Angeles Dodgers, 22-23, 24-25

Milwaukee Brewers, 26
Minnesota Twins, 20-21
Morris, Jack, 21
Morris, Jim, 26-27

New York Mets, 6-7, 9, 12-13, 15, 25
New York Yankees, 10, 14-15,

Oakland Athletics, 25

Paige, Satchel, 27
Philadelphia Phillies, 29, 30
Piazza, Mike, 22-23
Pittsburgh Pirates, 31
Posada, Jorge, 14
Puckett, Kirby, 20-21
Pujols, Albert, 18-19

Rivera, Mariano, 14-15
Ryan, Nolan, 12-13

St. Louis Cardinals, 5, 18, 19, 30
Sanchez, Jonathan, 29
San Francisco Giants, 4, 6, 28-29, 30
Seaver, Tom, 12
Smith, Lonnie, 21

Tampa Bay Devil Rays, 27
Texas Rangers, 8, 29

Weiss, Al, 13
Williams, Bernie, 14
Womack, Tony, 15
Wright, David, 7